RANCHER'S DAUGHTER

Dreaming Brides of California Romance Series Book 2

KAT CARSON

KATIE WYATT

RoyceCardiff
Publishing House
WHOLESOME INSPIRATIONAL ROMANCE

Copyright © 2020 by Kat Carson

Copyright © 2020 by Katie Wyatt

All rights reserved.

No part of this book may be reproduced in any form or by any electronic or mechanical means, including information storage and retrieval systems, without written permission from the author, except for the use of brief quotations in a book review.

Dear Reader,

It is our utmost pleasure and privilege to bring these wonderful stories to you. I am so very proud of our amazing team of writers and the delight they continually bring us all with their beautiful clean and wholesome tales of, faith, courage, and love.

What is a book's lone purpose if not to be read and enjoyed? Therefore, you, dear reader, are the key to fulfilling that purpose and unlocking the treasures that lie within the pages of this book.

NEWSLETTER SIGN UP GET FREE BOOKS!

http:/katieWyattBooks.com/readersgroup

THANK YOU FOR CHOOSING A INSPIRATIONAL READS BY ROYCE CARDIFF PUBLISHING HOUSE.

CONTENTS

A PERSONAL WORD FROM KAT

I LOVE WRITING ABOUT DERIVED FROM ACTUAL historical facts and events and sometimes individuals with interesting characters in nature that will captivate you and leave you in awe with the twists and turns of every story.

Packed with action, humor, challenge, and adventure her short stories will stretch the limits of your imagination, allowing you to marvel at the fascinating time in US history.

Thank you for being a loyal reader.

Kat

DREAMING BRIDES OF CALIFORNIA ROMANCE

Book 1: Fires of the Heart

Book 2: Rancher's Daughter

Book 3: Harvest of Love

CHAPTER 1
THE DECREE

MIDSUMMER 1878 – TEXAS

"MALLORY MAE DONAHUE! WHAT IN HEAVEN'S NAME were you *thinking*?"

Mallory closed her eyes and counted to ten as her mother rushed into her room with a frown, hands on her hips, followed by her older brother with a similar expression. The doctor had just left after having bandaged her badly sprained right knee.

Before she even had a chance to explain that the accident wasn't her fault, her brother Josh step closer to the bed, glaring down at her. She knew him well enough to know he wasn't really angry, perturbed maybe, but not angry. Maybe worried. And slightly exasperated.

He shook his head. "Mallory, I know that you're tough, you're strong, and there's no doubt you're great with the horses and the livestock, but one of these days, you're going to really hurt yourself."

"You need to grow up and stop being such a tomboy," her mother commented, her angry expression morphing into concern as she gently sat down on the bed next to Mallory.

Mallory sat upright, her back cushioned against the wall by pillows, another one underneath her injured knee. She knew that it was better to remain silent, at least for the moment. It was another hot Texas day on their ranch, and she had been spending the morning doing what she usually did, riding her horse, tracking down stray cattle, coaxing them to willingly follow her back to the herd, roping them if they didn't. This morning she had gone looking for a lost calf, found it, and held it in her arms as she rode her horse back to the rest of the herd. She had just completed that task and mounted her horse once more, fully intending to head home when a telltale rattle had spooked Jezebel, her horse. The mare had taken off, dumping an unprepared Mallory into the dirt, where she'd landed hard and twisted her knee.

Mallory had quickly retrieved the small derringer she kept tucked into the waistband of her trousers and fired a shot at the snake, which had been enough to scare the thing off. She'd hobbled along for a while, whistling for her horse, who'd finally returned, head hanging low in apology ... or shame, she wasn't sure which. By the time Mallory got back to the ranch, her mother and brother were fit to be tied. Of course, she didn't tell them how she had fallen off the horse, just that she had taken a spill.

"Mallory," her mother pleaded. "When are you going to start dressing like a lady? You're twenty years old and it's way past time you found a husband and started thinking about raising a family of your own."

Mallory made a face. Why didn't her mother or brother understand that women's work, housekeeping, and bearing children were not her primary interest? She had other, more exciting things to do. Since her father died and her brother had inherited the ranch, things had been rough. Her brother was struggling to find his own place as owner while her mother grieved heavily for her husband. Mallory felt caught in the middle in regard to her own emotions.

She saw the glance Josh exchanged with their mother and narrowed her eyes. Something was coming, she knew it.

"Mallory," Josh said, stepping closer to the bed, hands shoved deep into his pockets. "We've already lost Pa and we don't want to lose you too."

Mallory frowned. "I'm not going anywhere, Josh. I just got tossed, that's all, nothing to worry about." She gestured to her knee. "Doc said I'll be up and around in just a couple of days."

Her mother shook her head. "Things have got to change, Mallory. You've got to grow up, to stop being so stubborn, and start acting like—"

Josh interrupted, his voice firmer, a look of resolve on his features. "Mallory, we've discussed this. This latest accident of yours is unacceptable. You can't keep riding around like—"

"Like what?" she challenged her brother. "What are you trying to tell me?"

He heaved a put-upon sigh. "I'm telling you, Mallory, that while you're always welcome to live here, you can't be out doing men's work anymore—"

Mallory felt her temper rising. Her heart pounded. "That is so old-fashioned, Josh! I can ride, rope, brand, and break horses just as well as any man on this ranch and you know it! There's no reason—"

"I've made my decision, Mal. No more. You want to live here, you've got to live by my rules."

Mallory scowled, glancing between her brother and mother, who seemed to agree with Josh. "I can't believe this," she grumbled. She eyed her brother. "Are you telling me that if I don't stay close to the house, wear a dress, do laundry, slave over a hot stove all day to feed you, or sit in a rocking chair to mend your socks, that I can't live here anymore?"

"That's not what—"

Her mother broke in. "It's high time you put into practice all the skills I've taught you over the years, Mallory. They are necessary to find a husband and raise a family—"

"What if I don't want a husband? Or a family!" she argued. Her mother's eyes widened in horror and Josh groaned.

"Mallory, you know what the Good Book says. *Obey your parents in all things, for this is well-pleasing to the Lord.*"

"Please stop, both of you," Josh broke in. "Mallory, all I'm telling you is that you're not a cowboy," he said. "You're not one of the hands on this ranch. You're not to do the men's work anymore, understood? That's what I pay *them* for!"

No, she didn't understand. Tears warmed her eyes, but she refused to let either of them see. Mallory turned her head toward the window, blinking, forcing those blasted tears to stay where they belonged. She didn't say another word. Her mother placed her soft hand on Mallory's shoulder but didn't say anything. Finally, Mallory's mother and Josh both left the room.

Furious and hurt beyond belief, Mallory stared out the window. Already bored with lying abed, she cast her gaze about her room. Beside her brass bed frame stood a small side table with a kerosene lamp and a week-old newspaper from Dallas that Doc had brought with him and left for her in case she wanted some reading material. He'd grinned as he said it, knowing very well that Mallory Donahue was not one to usually sit around reading. Another washbasin and small water pitcher sat on another small table on the other side of her bed. A small dresser and an even smaller desk took up the opposite wall, pegs pounded into the walls bearing her hat, a spare pair of trousers, and a woolen coat for cooler weather.

Out of sheer boredom and frustration, she reached for the folded newspaper that Doc had left. She grunted, opened the pages with a snarl, and glanced at headlines and news articles, skimming impatiently, trying to distract herself from her brother's annoying edict. Who the heck did he think he was, bossing her around like that, giving her such an ultimatum?

Finally, growing more frustrated and annoyed by the minute, she flipped the pages until she got to the second to last page. Advertisements and personal ads. She skimmed, her anger building until she noticed a small column with an odd heading, "Mail Order Brides." What the heck were mail order brides? As she began to read the ads, she realized. Apparently, men placed ads for women to marry. She snorted. A man had to be pretty desperate to place an ad like that, didn't he?

She laughed out loud as she read the first one. "*Sixty-year-old man lookin' fer wife. Must be twenty to thirty years old. Willing to werk hard in gold-mine country. Will provide shelter, food, and two bits a month for clothing and such. Reply Zebulun Blake, Seattle, Washington.*"

"Ha, good luck with that, old man," she muttered.

She read two other personals that were just as bad. If a man was so desperate for a wife he had to place an ad in a newspaper, why did he think he could demand specific attributes such as being young, easy on the eyes, no children, or what have you?

She sighed heavily, glancing at the last ad. "*Twenty-five-year-old small ranch owner in Maple Grove, California. Looking for wife and helpmate. Age negotiable. Reply Jake Vance, Maple Grove, California.*"

She snorted again. Age negotiable? Even so, that ad was slightly better than the others. He owned a small ranch in California. Mallory was only five years younger than him and an experienced rancher's daughter, in addition to being able to offer a number of skills that would prove beneficial to any rancher, even if her brother didn't appreciate them.

On a whim, and still incredibly annoyed with Josh and her mother, Mallory impulsively decided to answer Jake Vance's mail order bride ad. They wanted to see stubborn? Mallory Mae Donahue could dig in her boots deeper than any man she'd ever met. They would see stubborn if it was the last thing she did!

CHAPTER 2
A LEAP OF FAITH

"WELL, IT'S TOO LATE TO CHANGE MY MIND NOW," JAKE said to his good friend Aiden as they sat on their horses overlooking the pine-studded hills before them, roughly ten miles east of Maple Grove. "She's already on her way."

"Did you tell her you bought the ranch a couple months ago?" Aiden thought for a moment. "That would've been right about the time you started writing her, isn't that right? I know at our wedding that you told me you had already placed an ad."

Jake grinned as he looked at his friend. "Well, it obviously worked out for you, so I was hoping the same for me. How's Gabrielle feeling?"

Aiden shrugged, then added a grimace. "Dealing with morning sickness, but otherwise fine. "She's doing the exercises that Doc gave her and we're seeing some improvement."

Aiden had placed an ad for a mail order bride in early summer. Gabrielle had come from Missouri after losing her parents in a tragic fire that had also caused terrible burns on her hands and arms and was still working on increasing her mobility.

"Did you tell her that you own the mercantile?"

Again, Jake shook his head. "No, I just told her I had a small ranch. You know that's always been my goal. The mercantile just brings in some extra money that I can use someday to increase the property boundaries."

"I wish you well with that," Aiden said, meaning it. "But don't forget you're getting awful close to land owned by Marley Bascom."

Jake snorted in disgust. Marley Bascom was what most people around here called a land baron. Of English descent, the man was greedy. He owned at least five thousand acres of land to the north and east, much of it spreading over timberland. As it was, he owned nearly half of the valley in which the town of Maple Grove lay. He ran a huge herd of cattle but made most of his money in timber.

"Well, there's one parcel that I know he won't get," Jake said. "My fifty acres." Owning property and having a ranch of his own had been a lifelong dream for Jake. He had also done fairly well with the mercantile. He wasn't money hungry like Bascom. He just wanted stability. He wanted to earn and save enough money to be self-sufficient and not worry about what might happen tomorrow.

Growing up an orphan, he'd never really had a chance to focus on anything other than survival. Even now, as a thirty-year-old, he lived and worked day in and day out, always worried that he might lose what he'd worked so hard for. After all, it had happened to his parents when he was a lad. They'd lost everything they had due to an accident that had left his parents so far in debt they could never climb their way out. They had all ended up in a poor house in northeastern Pennsylvania. His parents had died there, broken in spirit and soul. When he was thirteen years old, Jake had struck out on his own and had been looking out for himself ever since.

Jake had leaned heavily on his faith after his parents died. As far as he was concerned, the only thing he could truly rely on in his life was God. Sure, He worked in mysterious ways, but Jake felt that He was always there, come good times or bad. Before she had passed, his mother had repeatedly read to him from the second book of Samuel in the Bible. Jake always remembered one of her favorite passages. *"The Lord is my rock, my fortress and my deliverer; the God of my strength, in Him I will trust. My shield and the horn of my salvation, my stronghold and my refuge ..."*

"You know, Jake, I learned the hard way with Gabrielle. It pays to be honest from the get-go."

Jake was familiar with Aiden's story. Aiden had lost his wife, Sarah, leaving his two young children without a mother. He had placed an ad for a mail order bride, but not for love. He just wanted someone to help take care of the kids and basically take care of him too. Jake smiled. Not exactly the way things had turned out, and Aiden and

Gabrielle had had some challenges, but now the two of them were deeply in love, happy, and settled.

Jake had followed suit and placed an ad as well. While he hadn't really expected a reply, he had received the first letter with a wink and a grin from the postmaster.

"So what's she like?"

Jake thought about the few letters that he had exchanged with Mallory Mae Donahue. "Well, she grew up on a ranch in Texas. Her father died and her older brother now owns and runs the ranch. She and her mother live there with him."

"So if she has family and a place to stay, why did she answer your ad?"

Jake looked at his friend. "I didn't ask."

At Aiden's disapproving frown, he defended himself. "Look, Aiden, the only reason I sent for a wife was because, well, there's no one here that appeals to me. Besides, I need someone to tend the mercantile while I work on getting the house on the ranch finished and then I've got to do fencing, tend the livestock, and—"

"Jake—"

"Well, I can't do it all by myself, can I? I can't be two places at once, and you know that the ranch is my dream."

Even so, he knew that Aiden was right. Jake should've been totally honest with Mallory, but the fact of the matter was, she, for whatever reasons of her own, was seeking a husband, and he was available and not too bad-looking if he said so himself. Jake had courted a woman or two in the past, but frankly, didn't have much time to waste on such tomfoolery. He couldn't really imagine falling in love. He wasn't even sure if he knew how to love anybody.

She would be arriving any minute now by stagecoach. Mallory would have endured a long, tiring, and dusty journey from Texas through dry desert land and all of the Central Valley of California until she reached Sacramento. Then another stagecoach ride northeast to Maple Grove, nestled on the western side of mountain ranges that got packed with feet of snow in the winter. In summertime, the valley below sweltered. Jake had spent most of his adult life in Maple Grove, the town growing bit by bit every year. People were nice and friendly, although of course there were some bad apples in every bunch.

This past spring and early summer, several unsavory incidents had occurred, the most recent being someone setting fire to the town. The criminal had poured kerosene over roofs and lit them ablaze. Thankfully, most of the town had been saved, although several structures and businesses had been lost. As always, the people of Maple Grove pulled together and rebuilt and the town flourished once more. Jake looked forward to the future, to expanding his ranch, buying a few more head of cattle, maybe even some horses for breeding. Things were looking up.

"I've got to get to work," Aiden said, tugging on the reins of his horse and heading back toward town, Jake close beside him.

Aiden worked as a foreman on old Mike McGregor's ranch to the south, a large ranch in its own right, but not nearly as huge as Bascom's spread.

"By the way, has Cody mentioned he's got some livestock for sale?"

Jake glanced at his friend and shook his head. "No, but I should see him in the next couple of days at the mercantile. I can ask about it." Cody Maxwell was another friend of theirs. He lived on his father's farm just outside of town. Maybe Jake could work out a deal with Cody. While he was a bit short of cash right now, he had plenty of merchandise as well as supplies that he might be able to trade Cody for a pig or two.

First, he had to get things ready for Mallory at the mercantile. She could stay there until the wedding, which would happen soon after her arrival to avoid gossip. Jake intended for her to stay in the mercantile while he stayed out at the ranch, at least until the house was finished and he got used to having a woman underfoot. He shook his head, hoping that he hadn't just made the biggest mistake of his life.

At that moment, the stagecoach rolled into town, bringing a cloud of dust along with it. The sound of hooves, the creak of the stagecoach itself, the slap of reins and jangling harness and chains overrode Jake's heartbeat as the stage-coach pulled up across the street. A few people stopped to look, always curious about new visitors or those returning, but most went about their business. Children cavorted, running across the street playing their hoop and stick game while nearby, an older couple walked arm in arm toward the small restaurant beside the hotel. A bit further down the Main Street, a man dismounted his horse and tied the reins to the hitching post in front of the newly built feed and livery toward the edge of town.

Heart pounding even harder now, Jake watched a middle-aged, portly man step from the stagecoach wearing a bowler hat and a vest. He waved hello to Tyler Adelson, the banker, returning from a trip to Sacramento. His eyes never left the open door of the stagecoach. He swallowed hard as a woman's hand clutched at the doorway. He saw scuffed boots, which prompted a confused frown, and then a long, dark brown woolen skirt. A white linen blouse appeared next, and then her face. She was one of the prettiest women Jake had ever laid eyes on. She hopped lightly to the ground, looking curiously around. His eyes widened. Was this Mallory? His fiancée? He almost laughed. How could a man get so lucky?

He'd just started to cross the dusty street when an alarmed shout broke the peace of the morning. Both he and Mallory glanced toward the western edge of town from where the stagecoach had just come. Jake's eyes widened when he saw two out-of-control bay horses pulling a buggy racing madly down Main Street, a woman screeching, unable to control the pair as they sprinted pell-mell toward them, hooves pounding and kicking up huge clods of dirt, reins trailing, eyes wide with fright.

He stared a second and then glanced over toward Mallory, just now stepping into the street. He thrust out his hand. "Wait! Mallory, wait!"

Much to his astonishment, and at the very moment the charging horses reached her, Mallory broke into a run, not away, but *alongside* the horses. Jake couldn't see her past the horses, the buggy, or through the cloud of dust the charging animals kicked up. He yelled, afraid that she'd been trampled. He stared in horror until he spied a brief flash of white and saw an arm reaching for a dangling rein and, then to his absolute amazement, Jake watched Mallory leap atop the lead horse, hunched low, legs tightly clinging to the horse's barrel as the geldings, the buggy, and a screaming Millicent Jacoby careened down the middle of Maple Grove's Main Street.

CHAPTER 3

THE TRUTH OF THE MATTER

MALLORY'S LEGS CLUNG TIGHTLY TO THE BARREL OF THE racing horse. With one fist wrapped in a handful of the black horse's mane, she desperately reached for the dangling rein. If that leather strap dangling on the ground below the horse's hooves tangled up in one of their legs, it could be deadly, not only for the two horses pulling the large buggy, but the elderly woman screaming for all she was worth.

The heat and sweat emanating from the horse's back seeped through her skirt, but Mallory didn't care. Leaning forward, she spoke softly to the horse, soothing it, allowing her body to relax and roll with its movements though her heart pounded like mad. Not from the panicked horses—oh no, not them. She could handle them. No, she was afraid she hadn't made such a good impression on that man standing across from the stage as she'd climbed out. The one who'd called out her name. Chances were that man was Jake Vance, her fiancé.

It was chaos. Dust roiled around them; townspeople shouted; several men tried to run alongside the horses to help. The woman in the back screamed; children squealed; and the horses snorted in fear. Like Mallory, a couple of men tried to grab the dangling reins. One man tried to jump on the other horse's back but failed. She'd had a lot of practice over the years. She had tamed many horses, broken a few, and even learned how to perform a few tricks riding bareback. Her mother had incessantly tried to discourage her from doing so, but when Mallory Donahue put her mind to something, she did it, no matter what.

Keeping her grip on the horse's mane with one hand, Mallory leaned further forward, her chin nearly touching the horse's neck. She kept her head tilted slightly to the side, just in case the horse decided to rear its head. She didn't need a cracked skull on top of everything else. She leaned over as far as she dared, clinging tightly to the horse's barrel with her thighs and finally managed to grab one of the reins close to where they were attached to the horse's halter. She reversed the process and managed to grab the other. Both reins gripped tightly in her hands, close to the horse's head, Mallory pulled back, talking softly to the horses all the while.

Finally, she felt them slowing. Townspeople raced toward them, more hands grabbing for the horses and the buggy. Someone slammed the buggy brake down. Two people grabbed the harnesses. The horses finally came to a stop at the far edge of town, just beyond what looked like the livery stables, their sides heaving, blowing hard, and tossing their heads hard. One of the horses foamed at the mouth and Mallory felt the slick wet hide beneath her as the animal stood trembling. She continued to speak quietly to the horse, stroking its neck, then reached over and gave the other one a pat on the shoulder.

For several moments, she heard nothing but the horses blowing and their hooves stomping, still jittery, the woman in the buggy behind her weeping softly. Only then did Mallory realize those were the only sounds she heard. She sat upright, looked around, and saw about a dozen men and a few women staring at her. In front of the crowd stood the very handsome man who had called out to her.

Mallory swallowed. She saw more than one man's gaze take in her appearance, her hair now more than likely disheveled, her blouse dirtied and flecked with horse sweat and dirt, and her legs. She had the decency to blush when she realized that her skirt had ridden up to her knees, exposing a bit of calf before her scuffed boots hid the rest.

She managed a grin. "Hello," she said to no one in particular, though her eyes kept returning to the handsome man staring up at her in shock. "Would you happen to be Jake Vance?"

He swallowed, his Adam's apple bobbing as he seemed to come out of his daze. "I am," he said, lifting a hand to help her down.

Though she didn't need it and would've happily slid down on her own, Mallory didn't want to throw her leg over the back of the horse like she normally would, not with this crowd watching, and certainly not while wearing a skirt. She reached for Jake's hand, marveling at the sudden tingle she felt when he clasped one hand firmly, then lifted his other hand, placed it under her arm, and swept her off the back of the horse as if she weighed nothing at all. As her feet landed on the ground, Mallory nodded her thanks.

She pulled her gaze away from Jake's hazel-brown eyes and glanced at the older woman in the buggy. "Is she all right?"

Before Jake could answer, murmurings broke out through the small crowd that had gathered. Mallory caught snippets of words and comments.

"... saved Millicent ..."

"Who is she?"

A laughing voice. "... Jake's fiancée ..."

"All right, the excitement's over," a gruff voice broke into the crowd. The spectators parted as a man dressed in worn pants, an old, faded blue shirt, and a leather vest with a tin star pinned on it came forward. He stared at Mallory a moment and then belatedly remembered his manners. He swept off his battered hat, his overly long hair falling into his eyes.

"Obliged, ma'am," he said, gesturing from the horses to Millicent. "I'm Sheriff Andrew Flanagan. You okay?"

Mallory smiled and nodded. "Of course, thank you." She cast a not-so-certain gaze around the spectators, some looking at her with amusement, some with curiosity, and some with downright disapproval. She ignored them and turned back to Jake. He was certainly a handsome man, with lean, sharp features, slightly hooded eyes and a straight nose, nostrils slightly flared at the moment, and nice, full lips. A hint of whiskers covered his jaw. She lifted her eyebrow at him.

At that moment, Jake seemed to come to his senses and offered her his arm. He seemed befuddled, but then shook it off, glared at everyone in the crowd, and muttered an *excuse me* as he escorted Mallory toward what looked to be the town's mercantile. She wasn't sure why. Did he think she needed new clothes?

He paused to glance down at her, looking confused. She bit back a sigh, then gestured over her shoulder with her thumb. "Don't make anything much of that," she said lightly. "I grew up on a ranch, you know that. I've ridden a few horses in my time." Though a slight frown of disapproval appeared on his face, Jake said nothing.

Now feeling awkward and uncertain, Mallory tugged her gaze away from him. He seemed upset. Why should he be? She'd done what had seemed natural. Besides, that lady ... Millicent ... would never have managed to regain control of those horses. "I wonder what made those horses bolt?" she asked idly. Jake didn't reply. "Maybe a rattlesnake. Maybe a child's sudden movement. Horses that skittish shouldn't be used to pull an old woman's buggy, I know that for sure."

Again he said nothing. Mallory's hand rested gently on a strong forearm. She felt the bulge of his bicep as he escorted her toward the store. Her head barely reached his shoulder. He was a man of few words. A handsome figure of a man, that was for sure, but quiet, maybe too quiet. Her nervousness increased by leaps and bounds. What if this ... what if she'd made a mistake? Jake didn't seem any too pleased with her at the moment, but there was nothing she could do about it now.

He led her up two steps onto the narrow wooden porch before passing through the threshold and into the mercantile. Mallory caught aromatic hints of fabric, spices, and oddly enough, a freshly baked pie. Her mouth instantly watered. As usual, she spoke what was on her mind. "I smell a freshly baked apple pie," she commented, her gaze searching the store for its source.

Jake nodded. "Gabrielle and the girls made it for you," he said, his voice surprisingly soft but deep as he gazed down at her. "Her and the girls, I mean. Aiden and Gabrielle are good friends of mine. They have two little girls and a child on the way. It was their welcome gift to you."

Mallory tried to smile, but the blank expression on Jake's face prompted her to second-guess herself. Maybe he wasn't happy to see her. Maybe she didn't suit him. Maybe she wasn't at all what he expected, or perhaps it was her hair and clothes, mussed now from her wild ride down Main Street. What a way to make her first appearance to her fiancé, leaping onto the back of a runaway horse, making a spectacle of herself in front of the whole town.

Neither one of them said anything for several moments, but she shifted uncomfortably. Why did she feel such an instant attraction to him when he'd barely uttered a handful of words to her? She finally released her grip on his forearm and folded her hands in front of her, glancing around the store. "Looks like a nice place."

"It is," he said, still eyeing her. "I own it."

"Oh?" she asked with a lifted eyebrow. "I thought you said that you owned a small ranch."

"I do. I also own the store, which earns extra money that I can use to eventually add property to the ranch."

She said nothing. Again, uncertainty settled in the pit of her stomach. Here she was, at least a thousand miles away from Texas, amid a town full of strangers and a man that didn't look all too pleased to meet her.

"I need help running the store while I take care of ranch business."

For several moments, his words didn't sink in. Then, as realization dawned, her heart skipped a beat. She peered up at him, eyes wide and a frown tugging at her eyebrows. "You mean to say that you expect me to run the store for you?" He nodded. A heavy feeling settled in the pit of her stomach, stunned. Now she understood the situation. However, Mallory Donahue was nothing if not, as her mother often said, pigheaded and stubborn. She tried a grin. "Why don't *you* run the store and I'll take care of the ranch?"

Apparently, Jake didn't find her words at all amusing. He had just opened his mouth to respond when footsteps approached and a shadow filled the doorway.

"Jake, is this your fiancée who just arrived, the one that just raced down Main Street on the back of a runaway horse?"

Jake glanced away from Mallory and offered a short nod. "She is, Preacher Murphy. This is Miss Mallory Donahue."

He looked down at Mallory. "Mallory, this is the preacher, Sean Murphy. He's going to marry us in just a few minutes."

At that moment, Mallory knew she had just borrowed a heap full of trouble. Jake had said nothing in his letters about expecting her to play storekeeper for him. Then again, she hadn't exactly told him how much she did on the ranch back in Texas. They'd have to work it out, find some way to compromise because there was no way on God's green earth that she planned on playing storekeeper inside all day when all she wanted to do was enjoy the feel of the sun on her cheeks, the breeze tugging at her hair as she rode her horse, herding cattle, sometimes saving a calf or two, and if needed, taming wild horses.

Still, this was her doing. She'd been so miffed at her brother and mother that she'd jumped from the frying pan into the fire. Maybe she should've been more honest with Jake. Maybe he should've said something about her running the store to her in their letters. Neither one of them had been honest with the other. They had kept secrets, and this was not what Mallory had expected. She probably wasn't what Jake expected either.

Jumping Jehoshaphat, now what was she going to do?

CHAPTER 4
LACK OF TRUST

Jake escorted Mallory to the refurbished church near the pond at the western edge of town. The fire a few months agohad caused some damage after some flying embers had caught the shingled roof, but those embers had been quickly put out and repairs made within days. Some new shingles and a fresh coat of white paint had fixed the small house of the Lord quite nicely. Jake tried to maintain a blank expression as he stiffened his back, feeling the eyes of many townspeople on him and his fiancée, soon to be his wife.

Still stunned by his immediate physical attraction to her and her astonishing rescue of Millicent just moments ago, he also felt embarrassed. He was sure he wasn't the only man in town to feel that way. He should have been the one to leap atop the racing horses to save Millicent. But he'd been too shocked to move. Jake didn't know what to say to her, didn't know what to think. He had expected a demure, quiet-spoken, if not shy woman, and yet, here he was, escorting a spitfire to the church.

He could not ignore the look on Mallory's face when he'd told her that he expected her to run the store. A slight forward thrust of her jaw, accompanied by a flash of her beautiful green eyes. Jake didn't know her from Adam, but he recognized stubborn when he saw it. He didn't quite know what to say, his words suddenly tongue-tied, so he said nothing at all. He wanted to stare at her lovely features, memorize every aspect of those eyes, delicately arched eyebrows, and her nose and those beautiful lips, but that would be rude. Mallory was not at all what he had expected, not in looks and certainly not in personality. Jake had an inkling that he would have his hands full with her.

As he approached the small church, he saw Aiden and Gabrielle waiting out front, their children, Rebecca and Mary, dressed in their Sunday best as well. Things had worked out well for Aiden and Gabrielle, who'd arrived in Maple Grove earlier this summer. Now, only a couple of months later, they were a happy couple, she carrying their first child together, her hands resting protectively on the shoulders of her stepdaughters. As he drew closer, Jake saw Aiden's grin and knew that he'd heard about the "adventure" on Main Street just moments ago. Jake offered his friend a scowl.

Gabrielle stepped forward with a welcoming smile as she approached Mallory. "Welcome to Maple Grove, Mallory," she said. "I'm Gabrielle Roberts and this is my husband Aiden, and our children, Rebecca and Mary."

Jake glanced down at Mallory as the children offered small smiles.

"I'm very pleased to meet you," Mallory said, smiling back at the children and then at Gabrielle. "I take it that you have come to witness our nuptials. I also heard that you baked that cinnamon apple pie that I smelled the moment I stepped into the mercantile." Her smile broadened. "Thank you very much. I'm sure it will taste as wonderful as it smells."

"It's the least I could do," Gabrielle replied. "I found myself in your shoes not long ago," she confided, then glanced at Aiden with a smile. "If you need anything, you just send word. Aiden and I live on a small ranch to the east of town. He works as a foreman on the McGregor ranch."

"Thank you," Mallory said politely. "I will."

Jake noticed the glance she gave him and that lifted eyebrow of hers, as if suggesting something, but he had no idea what it might be.

"All right, shall we get started?" the preacher said, pulling a pocket watch from his long, black cloak. "I'm already running behind schedule." He gestured for them to move inside the church.

Jake once more took Mallory's arm and led her into the church, a simple structure that served double duty—a church on Sunday and a schoolroom during the week. Long benches, four on each side, filled the space. Paned glass windows were set five feet apart along the length of the structure. During the school week, the benches were stored in a small shed out back, and small desks replaced them. At the head of the church stood a desk, the only permanent fixture in the room, a small wooden pulpit atop it.

The preacher quickly stepped behind the pulpit and without any further ado opened his Bible as Jake and Mallory stood in front of him. Aiden, Gabrielle, and the children stood slightly off to the side to serve as witnesses to the event. Jake's heart pounded, but he tried to hide it from Mallory. Her own hand trembled slightly as she held it lightly on his arm. She must be frightened. He knew he was. He couldn't fathom it. Just moments ago, the young woman had leapt atop a runaway horse without a second thought, without a moment of fear, and yet she stood next to him now, trembling at the thought of simply getting married.

Nothing simple about it. Jake's stomach felt funny and for a split second, he wanted to shout out to stop the ceremony, but he had to go through with it. He barely heard the words the preacher said and he doubted if Mallory took much of it in either. Neither one of them had been honest with each other from the beginning, which was what Aiden had urged him to do. They would have to work hard to learn to trust each other. Trust. Not an easy thing for a man like Jake. He leaned on his faith. *Those who trust in the Lord are like Mount Zion, which cannot be moved, but abides forever. As*—

"Jake?"

He jolted out of his fog and realized that the preacher had asked him a question.

"Do you take Mallory Mae Donahue as your wife, to love and to hold, to honor and cherish, until death do you part?"

Jake glanced down at Mallory, then at the preacher, and nodded. "Yes ... I do."

Mallory repeated the same thing, although Jake didn't hear too much through the ringing in his ears. Before he knew it, the preacher declared them man and wife. Aiden and Gabrielle hovered around them, Aiden clapping him on the back, Gabrielle wishing them both well. At that moment, Mallory looked up at Jake as he looked down at her. Did she see the same doubt in his eyes that he saw in hers?

He prayed for strength and wisdom as he escorted his new bride from the church and back toward the mercantile. Jake sent a glance toward Aiden, seeking wordless advice, but Aiden merely grinned, shook his head, and wrapped his arm around Gabrielle's shoulders as they made their way toward their wagon in the churchyard. No help from that direction.

Jake gazed upward at the sky. *Lord, help me. Tell me what to do. I'm counting on you to guide me.*

Mallory walked stiffly beside him, both of them politely responding to the well wishes, grins, and sometimes chuckles of laughter as the newly married couple made their way back through town. Well, they were married now, and he was the man and she was his wife. She was supposed to obey his wishes, but Jake gathered that Mallory Donahue Vance was a woman who wouldn't take orders easily. She had already bristled at the thought of being in charge of the store, and he imagined her new role would be quite different than the one she had enjoyed back home in Texas.

He didn't want to hurt her, didn't want to break that wonderful spirit of hers, but at the same time, he needed help, which was why he had placed the ad for the mail order bride in the first place. As they stepped inside the building, he closed the door, locked it, and spoke to her honestly for the first time.

"Mallory, I need you to help me run this store. I can't take care of the ranch and run the store at the same time. That's the primary reason why I wrote that ad for a bride."

She looked up at him, slowly crossed her arms across her chest, and tapped a foot impatiently on the floor. She said not a word for several moments and then offered a stiff nod. "Did someone bring my trunk in from the stagecoach?"

Jake nodded. "Yes, it's upstairs in the storeroom."

"Fine," she said shortly. "I need to change into something more comfortable. We'll continue this conversation when I come down."

Jake watched as she headed toward the stairs, back stiff as she went up and disappeared through the doorway of the storeroom. Just a short while ago, the store had received significant damage from the fire that had been deliberately set just two months ago. The fire had destroyed half the town and caused some damage to a number of other structures, including Jake's mercantile. The repairs had set him back dearly, even with the help and generosity of the townspeople. Donated wood, glass, and shingles had helped enormously, but it had still taken a good portion of his savings to replenish supplies that had been lost. The store was a valuable asset to Maple Grove and he couldn't simply shut it down. He still planned to sell it one day, but for now, he had to keep it running, not only to sustain the town but to sustain his livelihood and his ranch.

Moments later, he heard footsteps and looked up, his mouth dropping open in surprise as Mallory emerged from upstairs. No longer wearing a skirt or a dress. No, his beautiful bride came downstairs wearing dungarees tucked into her scuffed boots and a boy's shirt, which, though it didn't exactly hug her womanly figure, didn't disguise it either. Jake felt both astonished and horrified.

"Mallory, you can't wear that," he stammered without thinking. "What will people think? You should—"

She approached him, hands on her hips as she glared up at him. "Jake Vance, you may be my husband now, but you've already asked me to take care of the store when that's not at all ... when that's not at all what I expected or wanted. I'll try to be a good wife and helpmate, but I'm warning you that you better not push me too hard. I'll wear what I want because I want to be comfortable. I'll keep your store for you, for now, but I will be comfortable doing it!" Her voice rose slightly and more than a bit sharply. "And if the townspeople around here want to gossip, let them! They can either get used to it or do their shopping somewhere else."

Shocked speechless, Jake watched as she reached for the apron draped over the counter. He turned and headed toward the door, feeling a headache coming on. He unlocked and opened the door as, with one last glance over his shoulder, he left the store, closing the door loudly behind him, leaving Mallory sputtering in anger and dismay.

CHAPTER 5

FINDING THE WAY

MALLORY STOOD FOR SEVERAL MOMENTS, FURY BUILDING inside her. Of all the gall! To be stuck in a store by herself, and on her wedding day to boot! She had no idea how to run a store. Jake hadn't told her anything! Her chest tight with anger, she strolled through the store, eyeing the goods, noticing that they were marked with small tags with prices on them. Well, that was something, at least. She also sensed that Jake was angry with her for her unladylike behavior and clothing. Well, he deserved it!

It wasn't her fault that she had automatically thought to jump onto the back of a stampeding horse to save the poor woman in the buggy from having a heart attack or even worse. Jake hadn't been honest with her. He had said nothing about expecting her to be a storekeeper. A storekeeper!

When he said he owned a ranch, she had assumed ... she sighed. Maybe it was partly her fault for making such an assumption, but at the moment, she didn't care. Her temper was up. She headed for the counter and the ledger Jake kept there and opened up the book. It didn't take her long to determine his accounting method, who bought what, how much each item cost, total amount due, a small stub of a pencil nearby. She could do this. Mallory could do her numbers, she knew how to read and write, and she knew how to count out money. But she still felt nervous, being in the store all by herself without any instruction or guidance.

She stomped her foot on the wooden floor. How could he just leave her here alone?

Her temper gradually ebbed and she took another turn around the store. Though annoyed with Jake, she had to admire his orderliness. Not only his bookkeeping and ledger but the placement and order of shelves and his pricing schemes. For the first hour or so, no customers came. Then a middle-aged man appeared, glanced askance at Mallory, and then simply nodded when she introduced herself as Jake's wife. He bought quite a few supplies; ten-pound bags each of flour and sugar, a pound bag of salt, some seeds, which struck Mallory as odd since spring planting time was over, but it was none of her business. He paid for it all in cash, down to the penny, which was good because she didn't know how to open Jake's small cast-iron cash register.

Later on, Aiden and Gabrielle and the children appeared. They made small talk for a moment, Aiden expressing his surprise that Jake wasn't there. Mallory felt she owed them some sort of an explanation.

"We had ... we had a bit of ... had a difference of opinion," she finally explained, keeping her voice calm though she felt a flush of heat travel upward into her cheeks at the memory. "He went to his ranch. He left me to watch the store."

Aiden glanced at Gabrielle, then back at Mallory. "Did he say when he'd be back?"

"I'm not sure," she said simply. "He went off in a bit of a huff."

Gabrielle laughed softly while Aiden shook his head. He spoke first. "Try to be patient with him, Mallory. This is all new to him."

She frowned. "Well, it's new to me too!" She turned to find the children eyeing glass jars half filled with all sorts of candy. Licorice sticks, peppermint sticks, chocolate pieces, and other penny candies. She couldn't help but smile. "Is it all right if the children have a piece of candy?" she asked Gabrielle.

Gabrielle glanced at Aiden and started to shake her head, but Mallory spoke. "Please, let them. As a thank you for the apple pie."

Gabrielle grinned and nodded. "All right, thank you. Rebecca, Mary, you may choose one piece of candy each."

The children exclaimed in delight and thanked Mallory. Rebecca chose a peppermint stick while Mary chose a licorice stick. As they enjoyed their treats, Mallory gazed at Aiden. "Where exactly is Jake's ranch located?"

He raised his eyebrows in surprise. "You don't know?"

She couldn't prevent her scowl at the remembered affront. "No, he left me here to take care of the store." She didn't tell them that she planned on setting Jake straight in short order. She could tell that Aiden and Gabrielle were amused, but she was far from it.

They left and another hour passed with no additional customers. Mallory spent her time wandering through the store, examining every product, every price tag, determined to show Jake that she could be a storekeeper even if she didn't want to. At five o'clock, which she figured was closing time, she turned the Open/Closed sign hanging in the window around and locked the door. She would make her way out to his ranch on foot.

She heard footsteps on the steps outside the door. The doorknob rattled and she turned to find Jake's face on the other side of the glass. He frowned, knocking on the door to be let in.

She took her time answering it.

"How did everything go?"

"Fine," she said. "Only a few customers, but you have to show me how to operate the cash register."

He glanced at the machine and then down at her. She knew what he wanted to ask. Once more, she crossed her arms over her chest. "Everyone paid exactly what they owed. Lucky for me, they came prepared, and down to the penny. You should've shown me what you wanted me to do and how to operate that thing. I've never done this before, you know."

"I know, I apologize," Jake said. "I got a little upset."

She raised an eyebrow.

"I didn't realize it before. Donahue. You're Irish, aren't you?"

"And what exactly are you implying?" she asked calmly.

He shrugged. "I just heard that the Irish can be stubborn." He eyed her. "Are you stubborn, Mallory Mae Donahue Vance?"

She couldn't tell whether he was teasing her or not. She stiffened her shoulders. "Yes, I'm Irish. Donahue is an Americanized version of Donohoe, which in turn is an English version of a traditional Irish name, Donnchadh," she replied. "The name goes back centuries. We Donahues are descendants of a tribe of O'Donoghues and our family branch dates back to the fourth-century Irish warlord Niall of the Nine Hostages."

Jake nodded. "Good to know."

She wasn't sure what he meant by that but didn't have time to reply before he gestured over his shoulder. "Come on, I'll take you to the ranch. I think it would be best if ... well, until we got to know each other better, you can stay at the ranch at night, and I'll sleep up there in the storeroom."

She frowned. Was that really necessary? After all, they were married. People would talk, wouldn't they? She shrugged. Since when did she care what people thought? They went outside, Jake locking the door behind them, then mounted his horse. He reached down his hand and slid his foot out of the stirrup. Without a word, Mallory tucked her booted foot up into the stirrup and he heaved her upward. She settled herself behind the saddle cantle, only hesitating slightly before wrapping her arms around his waist. Jake clucked at the horse and the gelding started to trot out of town, more than one passerby pausing to stare after them.

They rode quietly for a bit, Mallory trying to ignore the feel of Jake's body pressed against hers, the warmth emanating from him.

"Sorry we got off to a rough start," he said as dusk slowly settled over the landscape, elongating shadows, accompanied by a slight breeze that rustled the long grasses and moved the branches and leaves of mighty oak trees that studded the foothills.

"I grew up on a ranch, Jake. I can actually be quite helpful on a ranch—"

"Working a ranch is not women's work, Mallory," he interrupted softly. "You're a married woman now and I can provide for you."

She frowned. "My family—my brother and my mother— were perfectly capable of *providing* for me, Jake."

"If you didn't need taking care of, why did you reply to the mail order bride ad?" he asked, glancing over his shoulder at her.

Her scowl deepened and she answered without thinking. "Because my brother, who owns the ranch now since my father passed away, told me ... no, *ordered* me to stop working like the ranch hands."

Mallory felt Jake's back stiffen.

"You worked the ranch like a ranch hand?" he asked. "Meaning what?"

She shrugged. "I helped with branding the cattle, herding them, sometimes went looking for a lost calf, things like that." She smiled at the memories. "Sometimes I helped tame horses, and I've even broken a few."

He said nothing and she continued. "I could be a great help on the ranch, Jake, probably more than I could be in the store. You'll let me help, won't you?"

He said nothing and they rode the rest of the way in silence.

CHAPTER 6
THE YEARNING

SEVERAL WEEKS HAD PASSED SINCE MALLORY HAD arrived in Maple Grove, and still, Jake couldn't quite determine what he thought about placing his ad for a mail order bride, what he wanted from a wife, and most of all, about Mallory. Mallory was one of the most interesting, frustrating, unique women he'd ever come across, not that he'd had vast experience with women. Far from it. He knew he had to let go of his past, of his mistrust of people, at least when it came to influencing his decisions in his life. He'd worked hard every day to survive since he'd grown up as an orphan, inwardly terrified that he'd lose everything he'd worked for.

It wasn't just his financial stability he was worried about. It was his sense of self and what people thought of him. He'd earned the respect of the townspeople over the years. They trusted and relied on him. And Mallory ... she was different, no doubt about it. Jake never knew what to expect with her. It seemed every time he turned around, she surprised him. He had primarily wanted a wife to help him run the store. Maybe not the best of reasons to get married, but that was it. Now he realized how wrong he had been. Deep inside, he had to admit that he also yearned for companionship. When he'd seen how well Aiden and Gabrielle got along, how their affection for one another had grown, he'd wanted the same thing.

Jake could have his ranch, he could even have a store, and he could have money in the bank and some security for his future. But what did it all matter if he didn't have someone to share his life with? He was attracted to Mallory. She was a beautiful woman, but it was even more than that that pulled him toward her. It was her spirit and sense of excitement. She made everything an adventure. And an argument. Even so, he didn't want to hurt her or stifle her zest for life and adventure.

Jake knew she was still unhappy having to run the store, though she did it well, and he wasn't too pleased about the way she went about it, dressed like a man. He worried about his reputation. His wife was one of the most unlady-like women he'd ever met, but at the same time, she was so very special. She was a handful, no doubt about it. Jake hadn't lost any business because of her way of dressing, but he worried that people would lose respect for him or his wife if things didn't change.

They'd had several arguments over the way she dressed, and she'd won every single one. Would he like to be told what he could or couldn't wear just because he was a man? Did she tell him to put on his go-to-Sunday church clothes every day? No, he replied, he couldn't get his work done in his nice suit. Well, she told him that she couldn't stand skirts and dresses and frilly gewgaws and never had, and besides, britches and linen or flannel shirts were much more comfortable. While Jake could certainly understand that, it still didn't settle the matter.

Still, over the last several weeks, he'd begun to learn which battles he could win and which he couldn't. For now, he'd won the battle about her keeping the store. Mallory was having some trouble adjusting, and unfortunately, some gossip had spread through town about her, not just about her clothing preferences, but her penchant for plain speaking.

"What are you frowning so ferociously about?"

Jake jolted out of his thoughts, sitting atop his horse beside Aiden, eyeing the bit of pasture they had just finished fencing in for his milk cows, one which his friend Cody Maxwell had sold him.

"Nothing," Jake mumbled.

Aiden laughed. "You thinking about Mallory, you?" He shook his head. "She's something all right. A little firecracker. I bet she keeps you on your toes, doesn't she?"

Jake scowled at his friend. "You have no idea."

Aiden laughed again. "Give it time, Jake. I know she likes you, so—"

"How do you know that?"

Aiden shrugged. "Apparently, she said something along those lines to Gabrielle. They've become friends, you know. And your little firecracker is very good with the children. They like her. She makes them laugh." He paused, shaking his head. "The only thing is, now Rebecca wants to wear trousers." Aiden chuckled. "Gabrielle offered her a compromise. Until it cools down, she wears her dress and stockings, and this winter, she can give trousers a try."

Jake glanced at his friend. "You think that's wise? Encouraging her like that?"

Again, Aiden shrugged. "Gabrielle's thinking about it too, believe it or not. She said the trousers are much more practical than dresses and skirts for working around the ranch—and the kitchen." He gave Jake a serious look. "Especially when it comes to fire."

Jake nodded somberly. Everyone knew that Gabrielle had been seriously burned in the fire that had taken her parents before she married Aiden. She had also almost perished in a fire set by the as-yet-at-large town arsonist, not long after arriving in town.

"Besides, it's not that important what she wears, Jake. Most of the townspeople are getting used to her, and gossip will die down, and—"

"Jake!"

A shout from behind captured their attention and they turned to find Cody Maxwell racing up to the pasture, his horse in a full gallop, kicking up dust behind him.

"Jake! Someone just tried to rob the mercantile!"

Jake's heart skipped a beat. "Mallory!"

"Mallory's okay—"

Jake didn't wait for him to finish. He quickly prodded his horse into a gallop, heading for town, Aiden and Cody close behind. His heart pounded in fear for Mallory as he raced back to town. Another robbery? Who was behind all this, and why? He thought of his brave little wife at the mercy of robbers, holding a gun on her, threatening her ... a surge of rage rose deep within him and he spurred his horse faster as he headed for town.

By the time he arrived at the store, a small crowd had gathered. The sheriff emerged from the building, placing his hat on his head. He saw Jake as he quickly dismounted and rushed up the stairs toward the door and placed a hand on his chest.

"She's all right, Jake," the sheriff said. "She's a bit scared, but the thieves didn't get away with much. She told them there wasn't any money in the safe, and if they were going to rob the place, they should do it later in the day after transactions have been made, rather than midmorning."

Jake stared at him several moments, absorbing the comment, and then shook his head. "Foolish woman," he muttered.

Sheriff Flanagan smiled. "She's a handful, Jake. Good luck with that."

Jake entered the store, ignoring the soft chuckle of laughter from the sheriff as he stepped inside and saw Mallory standing in front of the counter, arms crossed over her chest. She tried to smile but failed. The moment he laid eyes on her, he stepped toward her and wrapped his arms around her. She sank into him, her own arms wrapped tight around his waist, pressing her cheek into Jake's chest. They stood that way for several moments, neither of them saying a word.

Jake finally released his grip and straightened.

"Are you all right?"

She nodded. "I was a little scared, but they didn't hurt me."

"The sheriff told me—"

"Jake," she said, looking up at him, her expression somber. "I want a gun. I can shoot, you don't have to worry about that."

"No," he said, not even thinking about it. Anger replaced the slight fear in her eyes.

She huffed, hands fisted on her hips. "First I'm told that ranch work is no place for a woman. So I come out here thinking I'm going to help you on *your* ranch, but no. I'm apparently a storekeeper's wife and this is my place because it's so very safe, isn't it? Well, if you really want to believe I'm safe, I want a gun. If I'd had a gun, Jake, they wouldn't have gotten away with what they got out of the cash register."

He stared down at her, his mind racing. His Mallory? With a gun? Sure, some women in town had them. And he'd seen her do things that had, before he met her, seemed impossible for a woman, but the thought of Mallory with a gun scared him. Not because he was afraid she would hurt herself, but because ... because she would be fearless. And fearlessness was a fine line away from foolishness. If she'd had a gun when those robbers came into the store, someone might've been shot, maybe even killed.

"Jake," she said, looking up at him, her voice trembling with emotion.

For the first time ever, he saw tears in her eyes. The sight nearly drove him to his knees. His brave Mallory, in tears? Jake softened his voice and placed his hands on her shoulders. "Mallory, listen to me. I don't doubt that you can shoot." He swiped his fingers through his hair, offering a short, unamused laugh. "I've seen you do things that I've never seen a woman do." He gestured at her clothes. "You don't dress like any woman I've ever known, and I've never known a woman to take a running leap and jump atop a panicked horse pulling a buggy down Main Street." He paused, trying to choose his words carefully. He needed her to understand that he wasn't criticizing her, that he ... that he what? He finally realized it.

"Mallory," he said, his fingers gently squeezing her shoulders. "Don't you understand? Don't you see? I don't want anything to happen to you." His words didn't bring her solace that he had hoped for.

She stiffened. "Jake Vance, I'm not a breakable porcelain doll that you need to keep on a shelf behind a pane of glass to look at and admire. I want to be *useful*, don't you understand? I want to matter!"

He frowned as he gazed down at her. He saw the ferocity in her eyes. His heart skipped a beat, but it wasn't in anger. "Mallory, you have no idea how much you matter." She said nothing, staring up at him as Jake again tried to carefully choose the right words.

"Don't you see? Your brother and your mother, they worried about you. They love you. I can imagine they feared for you on a daily basis."

"Well, that's not my fault," she said. "If I were a man—"

"If you were a man, they'd probably feel the same way. That's what love is, isn't it? Worrying about someone? Wanting to keep them safe?"

She stared up at him for several moments, then shook her head in frustration. "Then what's the point of trying to do anything?" she asked. "Our safety, our lives, they're not guaranteed. Why don't we all just sit on our porches in rocking chairs if that's the way we look at life? It's not living, Jake. It's merely existing. Breathing air. Waiting."

Jake considered her words. She was right. Nothing was guaranteed. Their lives were in God's hands. But still, he'd already lost so much. His parents, his sense of stability, his ability to control his own life until he'd come to Maple Grove. Was this truly the way he wanted to live? Creating boundaries, living by set rules and routines that didn't allow for any freedom? He sighed. He'd had several disagreements with Mallory over the past weeks, telling her that she should conform to societal norms. She had disagreed.

Mallory was a unique woman, and he should be counting his blessings that she was his wife. Maybe he was the one that needed to conform. Jake stared into her eyes, then slowly bent down, his lips touching hers. She stiffened in surprise for a moment, and then slowly returned the kiss. It was apparent that neither of them could deny their physical attraction to one another. He was sure she saw it in him as much as he saw it in her. Now if they could just come to a meeting of the minds ... unfortunately, they were both incredibly stubborn. Nevertheless, it was important to give a little.

After the kiss broke off, they stared at one another for several more moments before Mallory smiled.

"A small gun, perhaps a derringer, would be enough. For protection, you understand."

Jake sighed, smiled in return, and capitulated. He was beginning to learn that there was very little that he could deny his wife. Chances were, he would always find it that way.

CHAPTER 7
A STEP FORWARD

A WEEK HAD PASSED SINCE THE ROBBERY, AN INCIDENT which had frightened Mallory more than she had dared let on to anyone, including the sheriff, Jake, or Gabrielle, with whom she had become good friends. After proving to Jake that she could shoot—which he told Mallory that she didn't have to do, but she insisted anyway, shooting at a bunch of empty tin cans with a rifle—he had reluctantly handed her a derringer.

Compromise seemed to be their best way to get past certain arguments, so she had promised that she would not carry the derringer around with her, but leave it in a small drawer in the counter at the mercantile, promising only to use it with incredible discretion. She wasn't sure what Jake meant by that, but she'd agreed. For her, it wasn't about winning arguments. It was about being self-reliant and as independent as she possibly could even though she was now a married woman. Her vows had told her that she must obey her husband, but his vows had also promised to honor and cherish her. As far as she was concerned, those vows were intertwined. To honor meant to respect, and she yearned for Jake's respect.

Mallory also found herself thinking about him more and more every day. She knew how he moved, how he breathed, and how he spoke. She could now gauge his mood just by looking at him. They were getting along better, not butting heads quite so much. Gabrielle had encouraged patience and said that in time, Jake would accept Mallory's help on the ranch, especially with her experience. Gabrielle had also told Mallory that it wasn't just male pride or his idea of "a woman's place" that prompted his behaviors.

The town was on edge. Mallory had learned about the fire that had nearly devastated the town, that someone had tried to frame Aiden for not only thievery but murder, and that there had been a few additional robberies, then a brief lull until the mercantile had been robbed. Mallory hadn't been able to describe the robbers other than one was tall, the other a bit shorter and stockier. One had reddish blond hair, the other dark brown. They'd worn bandanas over their faces and entered the store so fast with guns drawn that she'd frozen in dismay, finding herself looking down the barrel of two revolvers pointed at her. She knew that even if she'd had a derringer, she wouldn't have used it. Not in that situation.

At any rate, things had settled down between her and Jake a bit. But this morning, as Mallory had several mornings this past week and the week before, she'd noticed Jake moving a bit slower, like he was sore. He wasn't eating as much, and his features had lost some color.

She'd suggested this morning that he needed to go see Doc Micah Harris, and of course, he'd refused. So Mallory had told him if he didn't, she'd hogtie him and take him to the doctor herself. Jake told her he'd go see him in a day or two if he didn't feel any better. Mallory knew something was wrong when he'd told her that she could help out at the ranch a bit, helping to feed the livestock, checking fence lines, easy things like that.

Jake had said it was time she got better acquainted with his ranch and its needs, but she knew better. Something was definitely wrong. That bothered her and she realized that slowly, she had come to care for him. More than a little. A lot. Even so, Jake watched her like a hawk, still stubborn and apparently reluctant to share any control. While she had a few ideas that she wanted to broach with him that might make a few of the chores a bit easier, Mallory didn't bring them up just yet.

Maybe his behavior was due to the visitor they'd had on the ranch a week ago. A rancher from the north, one who Jake disapprovingly and sarcastically identified as "the land baron," had paid Jake a visit. It had been close to suppertime, and as Jake stepped out on the porch to answer his hail from the yard, Mallory had hovered in the doorway with a frown. To her surprise, the man had foregone any neighborly greeting and abruptly offered Jake a fair amount of money for his ranch property. It was an outrageous offer, and of course, Jake had refused. The man had simply turned his horse around and ridden away.

Over supper, Mallory queried him about it. "Why did you turn him down? That's an awful lot of money. You could buy an even better piece of land somewhere else."

Jake merely shook his head. "I like it here. That man is Marley Bascom. He wants to own the entire valley someday. He'd like nothing better than to kick everyone out of Maple Grove and turn this entire valley into his little kingdom." He stabbed at a piece of chicken but didn't eat it, staring at it morosely. "Several of us have refused to sell out to him. Cody Maxwell and his father, who own a farm not far from here, have refused. So have I, numerous times, as well as Travis Bates, who owns a hundred acres or so to the northwest of town."

Mallory understood all that. There were land barons in Texas too, some willing to go to great lengths to get ahold of more and more land. "Is he dangerous?"

Jake looked at her with a lifted eyebrow. "No, I don't think so. I mean, all he's done is badger. He's never made any threats or anything like that." He gently placed his fork down on the table. "I'm not feeling very hungry tonight. I think I'll just turn in."

Mallory looked at him, hiding her concern. "Tomorrow morning, you're going to see Doc." He started to protest. "If you refuse to go see Doc, then I'll refuse to set one foot in your store until you do."

Jake heaved a sigh, then finally nodded. "You're a hard woman, Mallory Vance. A hard woman indeed."

She offered a smile that didn't quite reach her eyes as she watched Jake move slowly and stiffly toward their bedroom. Something was wrong. She knew it. Fear gripped her heart, and it was at that moment she realized she had fallen in love with the stubborn, opinionated, and ever-so handsome husband of hers.

❧

"WELL, WHAT IS IT, DOC?" JAKE ASKED IMPATIENTLY, Mallory standing beside him.

Mallory watched, hiding her concern as Doc Harris turned from the table bearing a number of medical tools and equipment. She recognized the microscope, where he had placed a drop of Jake's blood on a glass slide. Doc had been peering into the scope for what seemed an awfully long time before Jake asked the question.

Mallory knew that if Doc was examining Jake's blood, his odd symptoms were something more than a simple cold. Since he wasn't coughing or having trouble breathing, whatever was wrong with him didn't have to do with his lungs. Beyond that, she knew nothing.

Doc Harris straightened and turned, eyeing both of them. "I believe it's anemia, Jake."

"Anemia," Jake repeated. "What is that?"

"It's a type of blood disease—"

The doctor raised a hand to stifle Mallory's gasp of alarm.

"In most cases, it's believed to be caused by a lack of certain nutrients in the diet. In some cases, it's temporary." He paused, then continued to explain.

"We believe that anemia is caused by a lack of adequate oxygen delivered to cells within the body. While most types of anemia are caused by deficiencies in nutrition, it can also be caused by a number of diseases."

"Can you fix it?" Mallory asked, her heart thudding dully in her chest. She looked at Jake, staring at Doc with a blank expression. He didn't seem too concerned, but she sure was. This couldn't be happening. Not now, just when they'd started to get along better.

"Let me finish, Mallory," Doc said. "In Jake's case, I believe the anemia is caused by an iron deficiency. You see, iron is what carries oxygen in the body. It binds to a protein called hemoglobin in red blood cells and helps to transport oxygen from the lungs to tissues, where the release of energy occurs."

"He has been tiring out more quickly than usual," she remarked.

Doc Harris nodded. "Yes, the symptoms match Jake's, such as increased tiredness, some weakness, headaches, and paler than normal skin tone."

"So, can you fix it?" Jake asked impatiently. "I can't afford to be sick, Doc, got too much to do."

"Your case is moderate to severe, Jake. You're going to have to take it easy for a while until your body has a chance to recover."

"What exactly does that mean?"

Doc glanced at Mallory, then back at Jake. "I suggest that for the time being, you take charge of your store. It's less physical exertion—"

"But I've got a ranch to run!" Jake argued.

Doc gave him a severe look. "The more you physically exert yourself, Jake, the worse this is going to get until it resolves. You understand that?"

"I can help with the ranch," Mallory spoke up. While she had wanted to work the ranch, this wasn't exactly the way she wanted it to happen. "We need to get you better, Jake."

Jake frowned, scowling at both of them. "What do I have to do to get better? And how fast can I do it?"

"Well," Doc said, raising his eyebrows. "You have to add more foods that contain iron to your diet."

"Like what?"

"I'm sure you eat plenty of beef," Doc commented.

Both of them nodded.

"What about dark, leafy vegetables like spinach and broccoli?"

Jake made a face.

"Baked potatoes," Doc continued. "Kidney beans, peas—"

"So more vegetables," Mallory said, nodding in understanding while she glanced askance at Jake. "He's not too fond of vegetables. Meat and potatoes, sure, but ..."

"Let's see what happens if you add more fresh vegetables to your diet, Jake," Doc said. "That should help."

"How long do I have to wait to find out?"

Doc sighed. "I can't give you an exact time frame, Jake," he said. "But let's try that for three to four weeks and then I'll test your blood again, see if we're on the right track."

Mallory could tell by the look on Jake's face that he was not happy. She turned and reached her hand out for his. "Just for a little while, Jake."

"If you don't take my advice, you're asking for trouble," Doc said. "Your condition will only grow worse."

Jake frowned. "What brought it on so suddenly? I've always eaten the same kind of foods and nothing's happened before now. So what changed?"

Doc shrugged. "We're not really sure. It could be age, stress, or overexertion without proper nutrient intake, or all of the above. They all play a role." He frowned. "If you change your eating habits and we don't see a change in your blood or how you're feeling, we'll have to explore other possibilities."

Jake didn't pursue that and neither did Mallory. The thought of something happening to Jake filled her with alarm. She also sensed, even if he tried to hide it, that Jake himself was concerned about his condition. He acquiesced much more easily than she anticipated, although he certainly wasn't happy about it.

So, temporarily at least, their roles were reversed, much to Jake's frustration and Mallory's pleasure. She felt free once more, taking the reins at the ranch. It wasn't nearly as large as the ranch back in Texas, but she had a couple of ideas that she wanted to run by Jake before she implemented them. She knew she had to take her time with him, and late that morning, rode into town to bring him lunch at the mercantile. Maybe she could mention some of them then if she felt he was receptive and feeling better.

She told him her ideas, and after he thought about it for a while, Jake's scowl disappeared and he finally nodded. "These are good ideas, Mallory," he said. "I wish I'd thought of them."

He didn't say the words with resentment or impatience and she smiled. Maybe, just maybe, things would work out all right between them. She already cared about him deeply, and knew that she was in love with him. Hopefully, someday in the near future, he might feel the same way about her. Maybe someday he would understand that just because she was a woman didn't mean that she couldn't stand side by side with him, helping him with the ranch, the store, or anything else he planned for the future.

They shared lunch, Jake frowning at the sliced roast beef sandwich Mallory had made, with raw spinach leaves and sliced tomatoes in the middle. He looked at her with a raised eyebrow.

"Just eat it, Jake. You want to get better, don't you?"

He ate the sandwich in silence, only making a face once. As she was packing things away and preparing to return to the ranch, a man burst in through the door. They both glanced up, surprised, and saw that it was Aiden. Mallory was about to scold him for barging in like a bull until she noticed his expression.

"What's wrong?" Jake asked, standing.

"Rustlers attacked McGregor's ranch again," he said. "Killed one of the hands. Sheriff's out there questioning outlying ranchers and farmers." He turned to Mallory. "You were on your ranch property this morning, weren't you?"

Yes," Mallory said. "But I didn't see anything or anybody."

Aiden shook his head. "I don't know what's going on around here, but things are escalating. We have to—"

"Aiden! Aiden!"

Jake, Mallory, and Aiden turned as Gabrielle burst through the door, clutching Rebecca's hand. Rebecca's face was red, tears streaming down her cheeks. Gabrielle looked pale and panicked, her lips trembling.

"Aiden!" she cried frantically. "Mary's been kidnapped!"

"What?" Aiden gasped, stiffening, his eyes wide with fear as he reached for her. "What happened?"

Gabrielle took a shaky breath. "Just moments after you left, three riders approached the house. Mary and Rebecca were outside by the chicken coop, playing. I came outside and ..." she choked back a sob. "I went outside and there, right in front of me, one of the men riding the horses leaned down, grabbed Mary, and pulled her onto the saddle in front of him. And then they raced off!"

Mallory rushed to Gabrielle and wrapped her in her arms. She turned to Aiden. "Where's the sheriff now?"

"I don't know," Aiden replied. "He said he was going to question outlying ranchers and farmers about the theft of several cattle and the killing of the ranch hand on McGregor's ranch."

Jake spoke up. "Gather some men," he said. "We'll get a posse together and go after them." He turned to Gabrielle. "Which way did they ride?"

At first, Gabrielle couldn't reply, her face buried in her hands. She looked up, cheeks now streaked with tears. "I don't ... north," she finally said. "They rode north."

Jake stood, weaving slightly, the color draining from his face as he grasped the counter for balance. "Let's go, Aiden."

"No you don't," Mallory ordered. "You can barely stand, Jake. I'll go."

Both men looked at her as if she'd suddenly grown two heads. She groaned with impatience. "Jake, stay here. If the sheriff comes back, let him know what's happened." She turned to Aiden. "Come on, Aiden, grab some men—"

A number of men had already approached the mercantile, obviously sensing something wrong, and news traveled fast. That and the townspeople had been on edge since the town had been set on fire. Quick exclamations followed bits and pieces of the story about the murder and then Mary's kidnapping and before long, nearly a dozen men were ready to ride out to look for the outlaws. At the mention of her riding along, she saw the looks. The disapproval. The scowls.

"Mallory, you can't go," Jake said. "There's nothing you can do—"

"Why?" she asked, turning on him, then glancing at the others. "Because I'm a woman? Because it's not a woman's place?" Angry, she pointed at Gabrielle, tightly clasping Rebecca's hand. "You think that if she had the opportunity, she wouldn't jump on a horse right now and go after them?" She turned back to her husband. "But I'm going to go out and do what I can, whether any of you like it or not."

"No, Mallory, you can't," Aiden said, shaking his head. "They won't let you ride with them, and this argument will just waste time." With that, he rushed from the store.

Outside, she heard the men talking among themselves, coming up with a plan, mounting their horses, and riding off. Her chest tight with frustration, Mallory looked first at Jake, then at Gabrielle and Rebecca, huddling together. She glanced at Jake and then started for the door.

"Mallory, you come back here right now!"

She turned to Jake. "I've got to do what I've got to do, Jake. I'll be back."

By the time she got outside and mounted her own horse, the posse had already gathered and galloped out of town, leaving behind a cloud of rising dust. She followed but didn't try to catch up with them. She struck out on her own, recalling the deep ravine that stretched between the

McGregor ranch and the edge of their own property line. If she was an outlaw attempting to escape unnoticed after murdering someone and kidnapping a child, that's where she would ride. Hidden from sight.

She would make one quick stop at the ranch, grab a rifle, and then strike out on her own, determined to help find Mary. She had no intention of confronting a bunch of murderous outlaws. When she found their trail, she could alert the sheriff.

CHAPTER 8
THE LOST CHILD

JAKE DESPERATELY WANTED TO RIDE WITH THE POSSE, but he knew he wouldn't make it a quarter of a mile before he would likely topple from his horse. Frustrated by his own condition and infuriated with Mallory, who had leapt on her horse and disappeared in the dust left by the posse, he turned to gaze down at Gabrielle, clutching Rebecca close to her, the small child's exhausted weeping wreaking havoc on Jake's heart.

The mercantile soon grew more crowded as word continued to spread around town and outlying homes and farms. Older men, children, mothers, wives, and sisters gathered, hoping for news. Soon everyone knew what had happened. They talked about it and wondered who was doing these things.

Jake tried to take care of everyone, offering sandwiches that Gabrielle and Rebecca had made to keep themselves busy. Some politely refused the offer stating that they couldn't pay, but Jake insisted. This wasn't the time to worry about payments or inventory. Someone was behind this. Someone had ordered their town set on fire. Someone had ordered the rustling and the robberies. Someone had killed a ranch hand. Someone had the audacity to kidnap a small child. His heart ached with fear for Mary, and the look of devastation on Gabrielle's face broke his heart.

Jake was furious with Mallory's bullheaded stubbornness, but he understood how she felt. If he hadn't been so weak, he would've been on a horse right now, chasing after the outlaws. Why did he think that just because she was a woman, she would feel differently?

The hours passed slowly, one agonizing minute at a time. Gabrielle, with her pale features and red-rimmed eyes, tried to stay busy, refusing to go home with Rebecca. She needed to be here in case there was news. She insisted on dusting and reorganizing goods that didn't need dusting or reorganizing. She did whatever she could do to stay busy. Jake let her. While a good number of people still gathered at the mercantile and spilled onto the porch outside, others went home, shoulders slumped, shaking their heads, features filled with worry and dismay.

What was happening in Maple Grove?

Gradually, morning turned into a hot, dusty afternoon. Impatience and frustration were the emotions of the day. Late afternoon came and went, and soon, dusk approached. There was no more talk in the mercantile, the people still gathered there silently. Outside, they sat on the porch, staring into the distance. Jake approached Gabrielle.

"Don't give up hope, Gabrielle," he said softly.

She turned to him and offered a weak smile. "I'm praying, Jake. I'm praying that they find Mary and bring her back to us. The thought of ..." She choked back her words and turned her face away.

He glanced at Rebecca, who had fallen asleep leaning against a pile of grain sacks. Suddenly, a shout from outside rent the air. Seconds later, an older man rushed inside the mercantile, gesturing with his arm.

"They're coming back! The posse's coming back!"

Gabrielle rushed to the door, clinging to the frame. "Is Mary with them?"

Those inside rushed to the door and spilled out onto the porch. Those on the porch stepped down and into the dusty street, shading their eyes against the glare of the setting sun to the west as tired horses made their way toward the mercantile. In moments, dusk turned into night. Jake spied a dust-covered Aiden, shoulders slumped, riding with them. His heart sank. Beside him, Gabrielle wept softly, once more burying her face in her hands. Jake felt a small hand clasp his and looked down to find Rebecca standing beside him, her hand tucked into his as she solemnly watched her father approach the mercantile.

"No sign of them at all?" Jake asked.

Aiden dismounted and stepped toward Gabrielle, wrapping her in his arms. Rebecca let go of Jake's hand and rushed toward her father and stepmother, throwing her arms around both of them, sobbing.

Aiden turned to those gathered at the mercantile, tried to speak, then merely shook his head. One of the young men who had joined the posse provided information.

"We found some tracks heading away from McGregor's ranch and followed those to Aiden's place. We managed to find a brief trail from there, but then it seems the outlaws split up. We lost their tracks toward the foothills."

Jake's heart sank. Those that had gathered slowly drifted away, heads down, shoulders slumped.

Aiden spoke. "We'll set out again at first light, see if we can pick up their trail."

Jake said nothing. What could he say? What kind of encouragement could he offer? He had been certain, like the others, that the sheriff and his men or the posse of townspeople would catch up with the outlaws and bring Mary back. Horrible thoughts raced through his mind. Would the outlaws have ... what if they had killed Mary as ruthlessly as they had killed the ranch hand? What if they abandoned her somewhere out there in the wilderness? What if—

"I'm taking Gabrielle and Rebecca home," Aiden said softly. "I just—"

The sound of a lone horse approaching from the east prompted Jake to turn toward it. He figured it was a straggler from the posse, but they had come into town from the west, not the east. He stiffened and stared in amazement as he watched the rider emerge from the darkness and approach the mercantile.

"Mallory!" he gasped. And in her arms, she held a sleeping Mary, cradled in front of her on the saddle.

Aiden and Gabrielle turned at Jake's words and stared. Gabrielle offered a wail of joy and relief as she rushed toward the horse, waking Mary as Mallory pulled the horse to a halt near the steps.

"Mary!" Rebecca shrieked, racing forward.

Aiden stared at his daughter as Mallory helped her down, passing her into Gabrielle's arms. Tears of relief trailed down his dusty cheeks and then he, too, stepped forward, his arms going around Gabrielle and Mary both, Rebecca clinging to them, all of them crying once more.

"Praise be to the Lord," Jake murmured as Mallory dismounted and stepped toward him. He opened his arms to her and she sank into his embrace as he leaned down and kissed the top of her head. She smelled of horse, sweat, and earth.

In moments, shouts traveled once more through town, and it seemed as if everyone who lived in town hurried toward the mercantile, the good news traveling quicker than the wind. Laughter, congratulations, and cries of relief swept through them. Jake heard Mallory's name mentioned several times, and soon, the crowd gathered around Jake and Mallory. Though he desperately wanted to sit down, his legs wobbling beneath him, he stood straight and proud, holding Mallory close to him.

"Where did you find her?"

"How did you know where she was?"

"Why didn't the posse find her?"

All the questions came at once. Finally, Mallory broke in to explain. "The kidnappers left her in a cave a few miles outside of town." She glanced up at Jake. "You know that ravine that cuts through the back end of your property and then butts up against the foothills? I found a number of shallow caves in those hills."

"But how did you know to look there?" Jake asked.

Mallory shrugged. "I spent half my life tracking lost calves, Jake. Not much different looking for a lost child. I saw a single set of horse tracks climbing out of the ravine and heading back toward the valley. Who went up there? Someone who got lost? Or an outlaw? I figured it was one of the outlaws. The posse must have been following the main group of them, but I figured it wouldn't hurt to check out where the tracks heading into the hills led me." She gestured to Aiden, Gabrielle, Mary, and Rebecca. "The tracks led me to her."

As the crowd huddled around the small, reunited family, Jake and Mallory returned inside the mercantile. He was relieved that Mallory had found Mary, but he couldn't shake his frustration at her blatant disobedience and disregard of his feelings as well as those of the townspeople. Not only that, but he was struggling against his own feelings of inadequacy. His weakness, his illness that had prevented him from riding out with the others looking for the missing child.

"Mallory, you shouldn't have disobeyed—"

"Don't even say it, Jake," she said firmly. "I did what I felt I had to do. Just like you would have."

He stared down at her, his feelings and emotions in turmoil. Had that been meant as a criticism, a comment about his condition? "You mean if I wasn't sick."

Mallory gazed up at him, eyes wide.

"What? Why would you say that? Jake, I wasn't suggesting that at all, and to think that you would even think of such a thing … well, it's disappointing."

He thought about what he'd said. He was feeling sorry for himself. Instead of praising Mallory for finding Mary, here he was criticizing her. Still, he couldn't stop himself. They spoke quietly so that the others still gathered outside didn't hear, but she had to know how he felt, didn't she? "Mallory, you're my wife. Do you realize how embarrassed I was, standing there in front of all those people while you … while you brazenly … couldn't you see how they were looking at you? That doesn't bother you?"

She stepped back from him, her dirt-smudged face staring up at him. "Jake, I'm sorry if I embarrassed you. That was not my intention. But a child was missing!" she hissed. "Do you think I care one whit about whether or not it was *appropriate* for me to go out and help with the search?" She shook her head. "Such old-fashioned foolishness!"

Jake stubbornly folded his arms across his chest. "It's not for a woman to do. It's for the men of town to do."

"Fiddle-faddle!" she exclaimed, hands on her hips and eyes flashing with anger. "I'm just as capable—"

Jake stepped toward her, his anger rising. "Why are you such a stubborn, bullheaded, cantankerous woman? Why, just once, can't you do what I ask? Can't you—"

"Can't I what?" Mallory seethed, jaw jutting forward. "Why can't I be like other women? Why can't I be perfectly content to sit around sewing or baking, or doing laundry? In case you haven't noticed, Jake, I do those things! I do women's work! But that doesn't mean I have to only ..." She paused, looking up at him. "You don't understand me at all, do you? You haven't even tried."

He frowned. What was she talking about? Maybe he should tell her that he'd been worried sick about her, afraid that maybe the outlaws would capture her too. That he'd feared she would be hurt or even worse, killed. But he was so angry at the moment that he didn't say any of those things. His chest heaved with emotion, as did Mallory's, as they stared at one another.

What was Jake waiting for? For capitulation? Did he have to be the boss all the time? He stared at her, her high color, her hair covered with dust, the slight sunburned tint of her skin, and all of a sudden, all he felt was an overwhelming sense of affection. She drove him to emotions he'd never felt before, feelings he'd never experienced. Confused, still angry, but relieved that she was back, safe and sound, Jake stepped forward and wrapped his arms around her, her face pressed against his chest.

For a moment, Mallory stiffened, but then she relaxed and wrapped her arms around his waist. "You're the most confusing man I've ever met in my life," she muttered softly.

"I could say the same for you, woman," he replied.

They stood that way for several minutes, not speaking, but together. No doubt their relationship had been rocky and would likely continue to be rocky, but Jake realized at that moment that he wouldn't have it any other way. He didn't want a wallflower for a wife. He wanted someone strong, capable, and confident. He had that and more in Mallory. He had a feeling that she would keep him on his toes, and would more than likely frustrate him to no end, but he smiled, thinking that maybe that wasn't such a bad thing.

He felt tired and drained, physically and emotionally. He gently pressed her away from him and saw her own weariness. "Let's go home."

She looked up at him, smiled tiredly, and nodded. "Can't say I disagree with—"

Footsteps coming up the porch steps captured both their attention and they turned as the sheriff entered. His clothes covered with dust, he, too, appeared weary and sunburned. He gave Jake a nod and turned to Mallory.

"Heard you found the girl," he said.

She nodded.

"Do you think you could find the point where that lone rider broke off from the others? He must have been the one that had Mary, took off, and hid her in a cave. Poor little tyke must've been terrified." He muttered a vehement oath.

Mallory frowned, looked up at Jake, and then nodded. "I think I can find it again. I picked up his trail leaving the ravine. I didn't follow them to the west, but continued into the hills to see where he'd come from."

The sheriff looked at Jake. "Mind if we borrow your wife for a little while again tomorrow morning? I'm hoping that she can show us where that is and we might be able to follow it to where the outlaws are hiding."

"What makes you think they're hiding?" Jake asked, not liking this idea one bit.

The sheriff removed his hat and slapped it against his thigh, creating a small cloud of dust, watching as silt settled on the floor by his scuffed boots. "Sorry." He placed his hat back on his head. "Whatever's going on around here, it's gotta be coming from nearby. At least within the county. I'm thinking that someone's giving instruction to these outlaws and that they could be local."

"This is a big valley, Sheriff, and the county ranges hundreds of square miles."

The sheriff nodded. "I know that, Jake. But these outlaws have been a step ahead of me for months. First the cattle rustling at the McGregor ranch, now the killing. The robberies, the fire, and then little Mary's kidnapping. It's got to stop. We've got to catch them."

Jake knew that what the sheriff said was true, but the thought of Mallory going out again in the morning ... "I'll come along."

"No, you won't," Sheriff Flanagan said. "Doc told me that you had to take it easy, that you had a condition that could get worse if you don't do as he says."

Jake scowled. "Now hold on just a moment," he argued. "For one, Doc has got no call to be talking about me to others. Besides that, I can sit on a horse without exerting myself!"

The sheriff sighed. "I won't dispute any of that, Jake, but I'm not willing to take the responsibility of you keeling over and knocking your thick skull on a rock when you do, whether you think you can do it or not. I just need to borrow your wife for a little while. She can show us where the trail is and then I'll send her back home. We'll take it from there."

Jake peered down at Mallory. She looked up at him. What, no argument from her this time? He finally heaved a sigh. He wanted this to be over as much as everybody else. He grudgingly mumbled his acquiescence. "Fine, she can show you where the trail is, but then she turns around and heads back home." He glanced down at his wife. "Understood?"

Mallory looked up at him, offered a smile, and nodded.

CHAPTER 9
ATTACKED!

MALLORY KNEW THAT JAKE UPSET WITH HER, MAYBE more because he was unable to join the posse rather than the fact that she was taking them to where the kidnappers had split their trail. She couldn't do anything about it now. She could tell the men in the posse weren't too pleased with her presence either. Nevertheless, she knew where she'd found the spot and they didn't, so they were stuck with her. She'd quickly ridden toward Jake's ranch, where she had stopped long enough to pull his rifle down from the rack above the fireplace. As she exited the small house wearing her usual dungarees, boots, long-sleeved linen shirt and cloth vest, and a worn and battered cowboy hat, she'd seen their disapproving looks on their faces—well, most of them anyway. They'd better get used to it.

About half of the twelve men riding in the group seemed to have gotten used to her unusual ways of dressing, even if many of the women in town hadn't. Mallory wished it didn't bother her, didn't bother Jake, but she knew it did. Still, comfort was comfort.

"Morning's wasting," the sheriff commented, sitting atop his horse.

The sheriff was polite to her, but he, like several of the others, couldn't help the brief look of disapproval they gave her. To them, Mallory was an eccentric oddity. She could just imagine what they were thinking. They couldn't figure her out, and maybe they didn't want to. She told herself that it didn't matter. But it did. She lived here with them now, in Maple Grove. Sooner or later, they would have to accept her the way she was or not at all. Everyone in town liked Jake. Maybe she just had to be patient. Maybe, in time, they would accept her not only as his wife but as the person who she was. Different maybe, but a person just the same.

She mounted her horse, offering no apologies for the slight delay. They were going after outlaws. Well, *she* wouldn't be. Her job was only to show them the trail. But she knew better than to ride off without a rifle. She'd carried a rifle or at least her derringer nearly every day back at the ranch in Texas, always alert for coyotes, wolves, or snakes that posed dangers to calves and cattle and men alike. She wasn't foolish, even though Jake might've believed that she was. She wasn't sure how she could convince him that she wasn't.

She was just ... Mallory. They had grown closer over the weeks, but still, something held him back from fully embracing her, body, heart, and soul. She wasn't sure what it was. She knew that he was unhappy about his illness and that he chafed with frustration and impatience. She knew how he felt about what he called women's work and men's work, but she had begun to think that he was coming around to her way of thinking, especially after she had pretty much taken over the ranch duties. Mallory wasn't trying to show him up, wasn't trying to compete with him. She was trying to be his wife. His partner.

Maybe one day he would see that. As Gabrielle had told her on more than one occasion, Mallory needed to be patient. The Lord had brought them together for a reason. She could've chosen any other man in those ads for mail order brides, but she'd kept coming back to Jake.

"So how far out is it?"

She glanced at the sheriff, riding beside her, and she pointed toward the foothills in the distance. "There's caves over there, where I found Mary." She pointed to the east, at the ravine that gouged a sharp cleft a few hundred yards to the east. "That ravine runs this way for about half a mile, and then jogs sharply left, over there, toward that stand of pines."

The sheriff nodded and dropped back slightly to relay the information to the men. Then he spurred his horse forward until he rode beside her again. The horses made their way through some scattered pines, the aroma of their needles heavy in the air. Clouds built up to the west. Rain was coming. Knee-length meadow grasses swam like waves in the midmorning breeze. A rock outcropping fifty yards to the east cast long shadows toward them.

They were maybe a few hundred yards from the stand of trees when the sheriff spoke to her. "We have the general idea, Mallory ... Mrs. Vance. I think we can find the trail. You might as well head back into town now."

She looked at him with a raised eyebrow. "You don't want to backtrack the tracks from the man who hid Mary? I'm sure you can find his tracks coming out of the ravine up ahead, but—"

"Thank you for your help. You go ahead and head on back—"

A rifle shot rang out in the air and one of the riders behind them yelped in pain, grabbing at his arm, now bleeding. Within seconds, Mallory, the sheriff, and the rest of the posse members spurred their horses forward toward the cover of the stand of trees, still a hundred yards away. A couple of shots erupted from the trees as well.

"Spread out!" the sheriff roared, his horse charging forward, his rifle in hand. "Forward and right!"

The members of the posse split into two, like a two-pronged attack, half of them heading toward the rock outcropping, the others toward the stand of trees. Mallory's horse kept pace with that of the sheriff as they headed toward the trees. She leaned low over her horse's neck, trying to make herself a smaller target. Her heart pounding, her mouth dry, fright erupting inside her, she nevertheless charged forward, not wanting to hesitate and be picked off like a squirrel sitting dumbly on a tree limb.

Holding his horse's reins loosely, the sheriff lifted his rifle to his shoulder and fired into the trees, three quick shots.

Mallory followed suit and did likewise as they drew closer, as did several of the men riding with them. Then the men riding behind them drifted to either side, charging headlong into the stand. How many outlaws were in there? She didn't know. The sheriff shouted barely heard instructions, the pounding of hooves and rifle shots echoing in Mallory's ears.

"Find cover!" Sheriff Flanagan shouted as they entered the tree line.

Find cover? Where? Mallory pulled her horse to a halt as soon as they entered the tree line, not sure where the outlaws were, whether she was setting herself up as an easy target or not. She quickly dismounted and slapped her horse's rump, but he needed little encouragement to trot away. She grasped her rifle tightly in her hands as she took cover behind a huge pine. The bark felt rough against her hands, the pungent tang of sap strong. She glanced down, looking for footprints, hoping that she wasn't right on top of one of the outlaws. It was at that moment that a gunshot barked. Her hat flew off her head as pieces of bark erupted, several pieces stinging her cheeks. She yelped and dropped to her belly on the ground. Mallory glanced at her hat, lying several feet behind her, a bullet hole dead center.

Her heart pounded so hard she felt sure it would explode. Her hands trembled. She tightened her grip on the rifle as she sought out the shooter. That hadn't been a rifle shot. The bullet that had nearly got her had come from a revolver. Other gunshots rang out. Several seconds later, Mallory noted movement off to her left. She quickly rolled onto her side, arms extended, seeking the outlaw, the muzzle of her rifle pointed in that direction. Should she shoot? What if it was one of the posse members? No, they wouldn't be coming from that direction. It was at that moment that he saw her.

The outlaw lifted his gun hand, his revolver pointed directly at her. Without thinking, without hesitation, Mallory lifted her rifle and fired. The man went down with a yelp, grabbing at his shoulder. Oh Lord, she had just shot a man. She felt sick to her stomach, scared out of her wits, but, eyes wide and movements wary, she leapt from the ground and raced toward the man, her rifle aimed at him as she approached. His revolver lay several feet away from him as he writhed on the ground in pain, gritting his teeth as he glared up at her. Mallory kicked the revolver away and then, still warily watching him, reached down and grabbed the gun, tucking it into the waistband of her trousers.

"Don't move," she ordered.

"You won't shoot me again," he said with a smirk.

"Don't count on it," she replied. "My hands are trembling so bad that I might accidentally pull the trigger again." She wasn't trying to boast. It was God's honest truth.

Shots echoed around her, both from the trees and a short distance away, toward the outcropping of rocks. Mallory continued to stand there, her gun still aimed down at the man. She wasn't sure what to do. She couldn't leave him here, to get away or attack someone else. She had nothing to tie him up with. Soon, the gunfire stopped. She heard shouting, and then the sheriff burst through the trees a short distance away. She saw him staring at her, then at the outlaw lying bleeding on the ground, then back at her. The sheriff grinned and shook his head.

"It's over," he said, stepping toward her. "We managed to capture several of the others and killed a couple when they tried to escape." He glanced down at the outlaw. "Where's your boss?"

The outlaw merely looked up at the sheriff, spat, and then turned his face away.

Within half an hour or so, the outlaws were mounted on horses, hands tied behind their back, the reins of their horses tied to the saddle horns. None of them had revealed the identity of their leader.

A couple of the posse members had been injured, but none seriously. Mallory found herself riding beside the sheriff once more. He glanced at her several times, and she finally grew impatient. She knew he wanted to say something. "What?" she finally said, exasperated.

He gestured toward the hole in her hat. "That was a close call."

She nodded, not wanting to remember how close she'd come to ... "Jake's going to be none too happy to see it."

"Give me your hat," the sheriff ordered.

She frowned, but pulled it off her head and gave it to him. Without comment, he tossed it into the grass while she stared at him, wide-eyed with surprise. "Why did you—"

"No need to worry the man to death," the sheriff grinned. He was quiet for several moments and then looked at her again with an appraising smile. "Jake's lucky to have you, you know that?"

Mallory didn't know what to say. She hadn't expected those words from the sheriff. She glanced around at the other men riding nearby and noted their nods of agreement. A huge sense of relief flooded through her and a great weight lifted from her shoulders. Well, how about that. She seemed to have proved her mettle to them and gained their reluctant acceptance. A swell of quiet joy filled her.

"Yeah, well, maybe one of these days, he'll realize that too."

The sheriff chuckled. "Maybe sooner than you realize."

It was a tired yet happy group of men that rode back toward Maple Grove.

CHAPTER 10
MATTERS OF THE HEART

IT WAS WELL PAST DARK WHEN JAKE, WAITING WITH others at the mercantile, heard the sound of horses approaching. Several people rushed out, shouting that it was the posse and that they had prisoners with them.

Jake hurried outside, a huge sense of relief flowing through him when he saw Mallory riding beside the sheriff. She looked tired but unharmed. When she saw him, she slid off her horse and hurried toward him. She paused several steps away, looking up at him with a question in her eyes.

He couldn't deny it any longer. He loved her. She was his Mallory. He couldn't change her and realized he didn't want to. Throughout the long, worrisome day, he'd realized that there were more important things in life than his ego. He swallowed his pride and realized that he loved her just the way she was.

Jake leaned down, picked her up in his arms, her feet dangling from the ground as he kissed her on the lips, right there in front of everybody. A burst of laughter and a few cheers rang out and he wished the moment could go on forever. She was his. He was hers.

"You're mine, now and forever," Jake whispered in her ear. "And I wouldn't have it any other way."

She grinned up at him as he set her down. Townspeople surrounded them, clapping Jake on the back, others thanking Mallory for her help in capturing the outlaws.

The sheriff looked at Jake. "You're a fortunate man to have such a wife," he said.

Aiden and Cody stood nearby, agreeing wholeheartedly.

"She may not be a traditional wife, Jake, but she's a keeper," Cody laughed.

"And then some," Aiden added.

Jake wholeheartedly agreed, wrapping one arm around his wife and turning to watch as the sheriff turned his horse and headed toward the center of town with his prisoners in tow, the rest of the posse following.

"We still don't know who their leader is," Mallory commented as the sheriff led the prisoners away toward the jail.

"We'll find out, sooner or later," Jake said, staring down at his wife's dirt-smudged face. "Sooner or later, the truth will be exposed."

He hoped he spoke the truth and that the town of Maple Grove could soon put the mysterious incidents behind them and move forward.

"I guess it's time to head back home," Mallory said as the crowd slowly drifted away, some of them following the sheriff and outlaws back toward the jail, others going toward their homes.

"No, I think we'll stay here tonight. It's late, you're tired, the horse is tired, and it's a long ride back to the ranch."

Mallory looked up at him, searching his eyes. "You're sure?"

Jake grinned. "I've never been more sure of anything in my life." They walked back inside the mercantile and he closed the door softly behind them, then turned toward her, his hands on her shoulders.

He took a deep breath and spoke. "Mallory, I've been a fool."

She frowned. "What are you talking about? You haven't been—"

"Yes, I have been. I've let my pride and my ego stand in my way." He glanced down, then looked back at her. "Maybe it's God's will that I got this illness, and while I'm sure I'll recover in time, maybe it's time that I eat my slice of humble pie. Maybe this illness has been God's way of showing me the truth of the matter."

"Which is?" Mallory asked, her eyes searching his face.

"That I love you, just the way you are."

"But—"

"But nothing," Jake said, his hands gently grasping her shoulders. "I mean it. I love you, just the way you are. I wouldn't change a thing about you. You're my wife. I want you to be more than that. I want you to be my partner and my helpmate in all things."

She eyed him for several moments. "You mean that, Jake?"

"I do," he said. "I let my pride get in the way. Instead of being grateful that I had a wife that can handle ranch work, herd cattle, rescue old ladies from runaway horses, or go chase outlaws, I ... well, let's just say that I've learned a valuable lesson, and I promise to never, ever, take you for granted again."

He saw tears shining in Mallory's eyes, the first he had seen since she'd arrived. A smile lit up her features and she placed her hand gently on his cheek.

"I love you, Jake Vance. I'll try not to embarrass you, but I can't promise there won't be times that I do." She offered a small shrug. "I am who I am, but I will try, every day, to make you happy, Jake. That I do promise."

EPILOGUE

ONE YEAR LATER

MALLORY FOUND IT HARD TO BELIEVE THAT A YEAR HAD passed since that day she had arrived in town to meet her betrothed, a man she had never seen before, a man with whom she'd only exchanged a few letters before leaving her home in Texas, hoping for a new life.

She had gotten that new life and then some. Jake had slowly recovered from his illness and was now healthy and strong once more. He had sold the mercantile and she and her husband ran the ranch together. They'd done well enough that they could hire a couple of hands, and they took directions and instruction from Mallory as willingly as they did Jake.

The two of them got along well enough, with some occasional bumps, but that was true for any marriage, wasn't it? The captured outlaws had been put into prison, none of them admitting who was behind the illegal activities that had hung over Maple Grove for the past couple of summers. The rustling, the fires, the robberies, and of course, the killings and kidnapping of Mary Roberts. As it was, the people of Maple Grove still lived on edge.

Still, as their first anniversary arrived, Mallory was focused only on presenting her husband with the finest supper she could muster. Jake had ridden into town on an errand but was due back any moment. She glanced around at the kitchen, wiping her hands on her trousers, hoping that he would be pleased. She had planned T-bone steaks, baked potatoes, and fresh green beans from their garden to grace the table. Cody had somehow managed to procure a bottle of wine from Sacramento for the event, and Gabrielle had baked a strawberry and rhubarb pie, cooling now on the back of the oven.

Everything was just perfect. She strode to the door and opened it, gazing out over their ranch, growing slowly but steadily. The sun slowly settled into the west, and from out of the glare of the setting sun, Mallory saw a rider approaching the house. She recognized Jake in an instant, the way he sat so easily in the saddle, loose-limbed and confident.

She smiled, her love for him nearly bursting from her chest. She loved him with everything she had and knew that he felt the same way. She remained where she was, leaning against the door threshold as he rode into the yard, then dismounted. He strode toward her, pulling something out of his shirt.

He stopped in front of her, a grin on his face as he extended a rolled piece of paper to her.

"What is it?" she asked.

"Your anniversary present. Read it and see," he said, his grin broadening into a smile.

Mallory unrolled the paper, scanned it, and then read more carefully. It was a deed to the ranch. As she read further, she blinked back tears and looked up at him. Both their names were on the deed.

"Now you're not only my partner but an equal and legal owner of the ranch. Happy anniversary, Mallory," he said.

She looked up at him with a smile, carefully holding the deed as she wrapped her arms around him, placing her head against his chest, listening to the steady thud of his heartbeat against her ear. "Happy anniversary, Jake," she said softly, her love for him boundless.

Several moments passed and then he shifted, leaning down toward her uplifted face, kissing her, the gesture tender. "Together, Mallory, we're going to build this ranch and not only reap the benefits of our hard work and efforts, but have something we can hand down to our children." He gave her a wink.

She grinned up at him. "Someday," she replied with a nod. "But first, it's time for supper. We've got some celebrating to do."

With that, arms wrapped around each other's waists, they entered the ranch house, closing the door softly behind them.

To continue enjoying Dreaming Brides of California Romance. Please check below

Kat Carson Dreaming Brides of California Romance

Royce Cardiff Publishing House presents other wonderful clean, wholesome and inspiring romance short stories titles for your entertainment. Many are value boxset and as always FREE to Kindle Unlimited readers.

COMPLETE SERIES
Sweet Western Romance

KATIE WYATT, BRENDA CLEMMONS AND ELLEN ANDERSON

Katie Wyatt box set complete series

Katie Wyatt Mega Box Set Series

❦

Thank you so much for reading our book. We sincerely hope you enjoyed every bit reading it. We had fun creating it and will surely create more.

Your positive reviews are very helpful to other reader, it only takes a few moments. They can be left at Amazon.

https://www.amazon.com/Kat-Carson/e/B01G333YP0

❦

WANT FREE BOOKS EVERY WEEK? WHO DOESN'T!

Become a preferred reader and we'll not only send you free reads, but you'll also receive updates about new releases.

So you'll be among the first to dive into our latest new books, full of adventure, heartwarming romances, and characters so real they jump off the page.

It's absolutely free and you don't need to do anything at all to qualify except go to.

PREFERRED READ FREE READS

http:/katieWyattBooks.com/readersgroup

ABOUT THE AUTHORS

KAT CARSON LIVES IN NEW MEXICO WITH HER TWO dogs, a horse, and 20 chickens. She started writing when she was a teenager and has never stopped. She loves the rich culture of the old West.

Some of her stories are inspired by tales from the local storytellers in New Mexico and what her grandparents used to tell her. Others are when she travels around in her RV camping, fishing, hiking, climbing and engaging with other interesting people along the way.

She writes stories derived from actual historical facts and events and sometimes individuals with interesting characters in nature that will captivate you and leave you in awe with the twists and turns of every story.

Packed with action, humor, challenge, and adventure her short stories will stretch the limits of your imagination, allowing you to marvel at the fascinating time in US history.

I recommend them for anybody who enjoys an excellent feel good clean and wholesome romance story.

KATIE WYATT IS 25% AMERICAN SIOUX INDIAN. BORN and raised in Arizona, she has traveled and camped extensively through California, Arizona, Nevada, Mexico, and New Mexico. Looking at the incredible night sky and the giant Saguaro cacti, she has dreamed of what it would be like to live in the early pioneer times.

Spending time with a relative of the great Wyatt Earp, also named Wyatt Earp, Katie was mesmerized and inspired by the stories he told of bygone times. This historical interest in the old West became the inspiration for her Western romance novels.

Her books are a mixture of actual historical facts and events mixed with action and humor, challenges and adventures. The characters in Katie's clean romance novels draw from her own experiences and are so real that they almost jump off the pages.

You feel like you're walking beside them through all the ups and downs of their lives. As the stories unfold, you'll find yourself both laughing and crying. The endings will never fail to leave you feeling warm inside.

www.ingramcontent.com/pod-product-compliance
Lightning Source LLC
Chambersburg PA
CBHW020623160726
47991CB00002BA/904